Susi Gregg Fowler

ALBERTINA THE PRACTICALLY PERFECT

Pictures by Jim Fowler

Greenwillow Books
New York

For Jacob and Nathan Soboleff
and Madeline and Abraham Levy,
practically perfect nephews and niece

The preseparated two-color art
was prepared with a pen-and-ink line
and halftone overlays done in pencil.
The text type is Kuenstler 480 BT.

First Edition
10 9 8 7 6 5 4 3 2

LIBRARY OF CONGRESS CATALOGING-IN-PUBLICATION DATA
Fowler, Susi G.
Albertina the practically perfect /
by Susi Gregg Fowler ; pictures by Jim Fowler.
    p.   cm.
Summary: Molly and her best friend spend
a summer building a tree house, but their
project and their friendship nearly end when
Albertina proves to be less than perfect.
ISBN 0-688-15829-3.
[1. Best friends—Fiction.   2. Friendship—Fiction.
3. Tree houses—Fiction.]   I. Fowler, Jim, ill.
II. Title.   PZ7.F82975Al   1998
[F]—dc21   97-34460   CIP   AC

Reprinted by arrrangement with Greenwillow Books,
a division of William Morrow & Company, Inc.
Printed in the U.S.A.

Contents

.1.

Introducing Albertina

"I don't want to move," I told Mom. "I like living with Grandma and Grandpa. I like living next door to Bruce and Kelley."

"We're not going far," said Mom.

"It might as well be the moon," I said. "I can't bear it."

Mom kept packing.

"I'll be so lonely," I said. "Nothing will ever be the same."

"We're moving, Molly," Mom said. "Get used to it."

I cried the day we left.

"It's only across town, honey," Grandpa said. "You can come visit every day."

"I'm not allowed to ride that far on my bike," I said. "You'll forget me."

"Don't be silly," said Mom.

"There are lots of kids around your new house," said Grandma.

"I don't know them," I said.

But I was going to know them soon.

Mom and Dad started unpacking the minute the truck showed up at the new house with our stuff.

"You can keep the baby happy," said Dad.

Walter was sitting in his playpen, drooling. "You'd better not get me wet, Walter," I said, glaring at him. He grinned and crawled over to the side of the playpen. He stuck his hand through the bars and made strange noises.

Watching my brother is a little like going to the zoo.

After a while Walter got tired of making silly sounds. He shoved his fist in his mouth and went to sleep.

"Why don't you go out and meet some of the neighborhood kids?" Mom suggested.

"Good idea," said Dad in the big, jolly voice he uses whenever he wants to talk me into something I know is a bad idea.

"Go on, go on," said Mom.

So I went. Up on Seventh Street, a group of girls raced up and down the block. They were whinnying like horses, leaping into the air and shaking their heads like ponies tossing their manes. Really dumb, I thought.

I stepped off the sidewalk and into their path. "Hi," I said. "We just moved into the big red house on Main Street. I'm Molly. What are you playing?"

The skinny blond girl at the head of the line stepped up to me. I gave her my best smile.

She smiled back. "I'm Violet," she said.

Well, that seemed easy enough. Maybe this move won't be so hard, I thought.

Violet started to walk away. Then suddenly she whirled around, yelled, and threw her leg out in a karate kick.

She didn't touch me, but the surprise nearly knocked me over. I stumbled, and I heard Violet and the other girls laugh.

"I'm the boss of this neighborhood," Violet said. "I go where I want. I do what I want. I'm tough, and I'll be watching you. Stay out of my way." She whirled around again, stamped her foot, and the whole group stampeded off.

Nobody had ever been so mean to me before, not even Kelley's nasty cousin from New Jersey, who'd made us all miserable last summer. "I won't cry," I told myself. "I won't cry." But I squeezed my eyes together really tightly in case tears tried to sneak out.

"Are you okay?" somebody asked.

I opened my eyes and saw that one of the girls had stayed behind. I quickly backed off.

"I'm sorry about Violet," said the stranger. "My dad says she's insecure."

"She has a funny way of showing it," I said.

"She's not so bad when you get used to her."

I didn't plan to find out, but I didn't say anything.

"She always tries to scare new kids," said the girl. "By the way, my name is Albertina. I live in the house on the corner."

She didn't seem like she was planning to do

anything mean, but I was learning that you can't be too careful. I gave her a good look, and I liked what I saw—a short girl with a big smile. Her hair was dark, like mine, but hers hung down her back in two tidy pigtails. We chopped my hair short because Mom couldn't stand the mess it always ended up in. Mom would approve of Albertina's hair.

"So tell me all about yourself, Molly," Albertina said.

"Like what?"

"How about your family?"

So I told her about Mom and Dad and Grandma and Grandpa and baby Walter. "We adopted him," I explained. "He's from China."

"Cool," said Albertina. "Now I'll tell you about me. I just live with my dad. My momma died and I don't even remember her."

"Albertina, that's terrible," I said.

"I know," she said. "But it does make me interesting, don't you think?"

I could see what she meant.

"Anyway," Albertina went on, "now Daddy has a girlfriend, so maybe I'll have a mother some day. Daddy calls me Pickle. Do I look like a pickle to you?"

She laughed like this was the funniest joke in the world. And when she started laughing, it seemed like it *was* the funniest joke in the world. I couldn't help laughing, too.

That was the first time I ever heard Albertina laugh, but it wasn't the last. And suddenly I knew living on Main Street was going to be just fine.

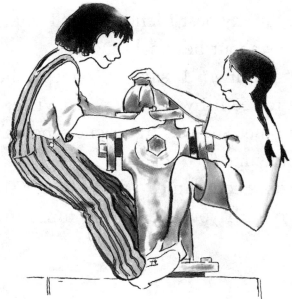

.2
Best Friends

"Albertina is my best friend," I told Mom and Dad at dinner that night.

"But you just met her," said Mom. "What about Kelley and Bruce?"

"They're my best friends, too," I said.

"Tell us about her," said Dad.

"She's funny," I said. "Besides, she stayed around to see if I was okay when Violet acted so mean to me. She was my friend when she didn't even know me."

"She does sound nice," said Mom. "Maybe she could go with you and Walter tomorrow to see your old house. I'm sure Grandma and Grandpa would be happy to meet her, too."

"And Kelley and Bruce," Dad added.

"Great," I agreed. "I'll ask her after dinner. She's coming over to play."

"Wait a minute. After dinner you need to do some fixing up in your room," said Dad.

"Dad!"

"Maybe Albertina can help," Mom suggested.

"Oh, sure," I said. "Don't you guys want me to have any friends?"

"Molly," said Dad in his stern voice. "With or without Albertina, you will work in your room."

Albertina surprised me. "I'd love to help," she said. She seemed to mean it, too. She even helped me make my bed. She made really smooth corners the way my grandma does. I could see that Albertina was good at a lot of things. I liked her anyway.

"Wow, a goldfish!" she said when she saw

Sylvia. Some kids might think a goldfish is a dumb pet. Not Albertina. I let her give Sylvia a snack.

"What's that?" she asked as I plugged in my night-light.

"Nothing," I said.

"It looks like something to me," said Albertina.

Now what could I say?

"It's just something my mom bought me," I mumbled.

"A rocket ship night-light!" said Albertina. "I like it." Well, that was okay. Maybe she wouldn't think I was too strange.

"I had a night-light once," she said, "when I was little." Great.

"So how come you still have a night-light?" she asked. "You scared of the dark?"

I couldn't believe she asked me that, so I just said, "Come on, Albertina. I'm not a little kid." I didn't want to be having this conversation, but Albertina wouldn't drop it.

"So why do you have the night-light?"

I didn't want to tell her about being scared of the dark. I wanted her to like me. I couldn't let her think I was a scaredy-cat!

"It's just something silly my mom bought," I said. "Don't make such a big deal out of it. You know how moms are."

Albertina didn't say anything. She just looked at the floor.

Suddenly I realized what I had said. I felt awful. "Oh, Albertina. I'm sorry. I forgot about your mom."

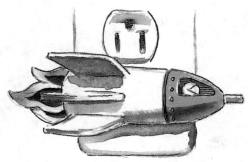

"It's okay," said Albertina.

But it didn't feel okay to me. I felt like I had to do something to make up for sounding so mean. I'd never told anyone I was scared of the dark. Nobody knew except Mom and Dad and my grandparents. Everybody thought I was really brave. They were right, too, as long as it was daylight.

"If I tell you something, will you promise not to tell?" I asked Albertina.

She nodded. "Cross my heart," she said, and she looked very serious.

"I *am* scared of the dark," I said. "But nobody knows. Not even my best friends. So please, please don't tell the kids in the neighborhood. It's going to be hard enough to fit in around here. I couldn't stand it if they made fun of me."

"Don't worry, Molly," said Albertina. "Your secret is safe with me."

.3.
Big Plans

"This is Albertina," I told Grandma and Grandpa when Mom and Dad dropped us off.

"Pleased to meet you," said Grandpa.

"We're so glad Molly already has a new friend," said Grandma. "Moving, even across town, isn't always easy."

Albertina nodded. "I remember when we first moved here," she said. "I sure missed everybody back home."

"You didn't tell me you used to live somewhere else," I said.

"I'm full of surprises, Molly," said Albertina.

She laughed when she said that, and we all laughed with her.

"Where did you live before?" I asked.

Albertina burst into song. "Oh, I come from Alabama with my banjo on my knee."

"Alabama?"

"Yep," said Albertina. "I'll tell you all about it sometime. Too bad they don't call me Susannah, huh?"

"Why don't you show Albertina-from-Alabama your tree house?" Grandpa said.

"It's not mine anymore," I said. "I don't live here, remember?"

Grandma laughed and ignored my crabby look. "If you ask me, it's still your tree house," she said. "Do you think your grandpa and I are going to use that thing?"

"Thanks, Grandma, but a tree house just isn't the same when it's clear across town."

"Can we see it anyway?" asked Albertina.

Grandpa handed Walter over to Grandma so he

could go out in the backyard with us.

"We'll stay here and finish making lunch," Grandma said.

I didn't think Walter would be much help, but I didn't argue.

"Wow!" said Albertina when she saw the tree house.

I told her how Grandpa had built the tree house for me when I was in preschool. "Mom was scared I'd fall out of it," I said.

"But I told her not to worry," Grandpa said. "I

figured even if Molly fell, she'd just bounce."

"Did you?" asked Albertina.

"Did I what?"

"Did you bounce when you fell?"

"I didn't exactly bounce," I told her. "The worst thing I ever did was break my arm, and that was because I tried to walk on top of the tree house. I was just a little kid then."

"You kids go on up," said Grandpa. "I'm going back to help Grandma with lunch."

"Wow!" Albertina said again when we climbed into the tree house. "No wonder you didn't want to move."

We sat in the tree house and talked about places we'd been and what it was like to move.

"When you came here," I asked, "did Violet…"

Albertina interrupted, "Did she welcome me to the neighborhood like she did you?"

I nodded.

"Sure," she said, "only I think with me she just jumped out of the bushes and scared me half to death."

"Then why are you friends with her now?" I asked.

Albertina shrugged. "I know she's kind of a bully—but she's fun, too. She makes up really good games, and she's a terrific soccer player. I guess when you live in the same neighborhood, you just get used to people. I'll take you over to

her house sometime, Molly. You'll like her."

"No thanks, Albertina. I think I'll pass," I said.

Nobody said anything for a while. We listened to a lawn mower in the distance, the little kids on the swings next door to Grandma and Grandpa, and the sounds of birds in the branches.

Albertina sighed. "I'd have hated to leave a tree house like this," she said. "But I've never had a tree house at all."

Then it hit both of us. She looked at me and I looked at her.

"Are you thinking what I'm thinking?" I said.

"I think so," said Albertina. "Could we?"

I nodded. "I think so. Let's go ask Grandpa."

We ran back to the house yelling, "Grandpa, Grandpa, come quick!"

Grandpa ran out of the house with a dish towel and a cup in his hands.

"What is it? Is someone hurt?"

Albertina and I looked at each other, confused.

"Don't look at me like I'm nuts," said Grandpa. "The way you came yelling, I thought something awful had happened. Don't do that again."

"Sorry, Grandpa," I said, "but Albertina and I just had the most wonderful idea."

Albertina looked at Grandpa. "We had the *same* wonderful idea at exactly the *same* time. My daddy says when that happens, it's a sign."

"Oh?" said Grandpa. "A sign of what, may I ask?"

"A sign that we should do it if it is at all

possible," Albertina said. We grabbed each other's hands and squeezed tightly.

"Would anyone like to tell me what we are talking about here?" Grandpa asked.

"Building a tree house!" Albertina and I said at the very same time.

Grandpa looked surprised.

"Why not, Grandpa?" I asked. "You could help us plan it, and we could build it at my new house. I'm sure we could do it."

"I'm sure you could, too," said Grandpa, "especially since you *both* had the very same idea."

"You'll help us, won't you, Grandpa?" I asked. "We'll need plans."

"Yes, blueprints," said Albertina.

"I see what you mean," said Grandpa. "Yes, I suppose I could lend a hand with design. I may even have a little scrap lumber you could use."

"Oh, Grandpa. You're the best!" I said. Albertina agreed with me. We were so excited we could hardly wait to go home and figure out where we would build our new tree house.

"Wait a minute," said Grandpa. "You can't go yet. Your parents aren't back, and Grandma has a good lunch planned."

"We weren't going to go this minute," I said. "Were we, Albertina?"

She shook her head. "That lunch smells just wonderful. I wouldn't want to miss any of it." She looked at Grandpa. "You might think I'm just saying that to be polite, but I'm not. I say what I mean and I mean what I say."

Albertina's nose told her right. Grandma's lunch was so good that we both had seconds on soup *and* seconds on dessert.

After lunch I took Albertina to meet Kelley and Bruce. Bruce was shy, but Kelley and Albertina started laughing right away, and pretty soon Bruce joined in. Albertina sure knows how to make friends. Soon we were all up in my old tree house, talking and laughing and making plans. We told Kelley and Bruce about building a new tree house, and they thought it was a great idea.

Albertina and I were still up in the tree house when Mom and Dad came to take us home.

"You two decide on a tree," said Grandpa. "I'll come over Friday night, and we'll get started."

"Yes!" Albertina and I said—at the very same time, and then we burst out laughing. We laughed all the way home.

.4.
The Fun Begins

"Which tree will it be?" Grandpa asked when he came over Friday night.

"This one," said Albertina, jumping up and swinging from a branch.

"Good choice," said Grandpa. "Let's see what we can figure out."

We spent all evening making plans.

"Tomorrow I'll bring over some lumber," said Grandpa. "I'll help you get the floor down. Then you're on your own."

"I can't wait," Albertina and I said at the same time.

Grandpa gave us a funny look. "You're doing it again," he said.

We all laughed, and Grandpa hugged us both good-bye.

Dad said I could walk Albertina home since it was still light outside.

We walked arm in arm, talking and laughing, when suddenly the bushes near us trembled. We grabbed each other as the bushes began shaking. Then, with a shout, out jumped Violet.

"Ta da!" she shrieked. I shrank back, keeping my eyes on her karate-kicking legs. Albertina just laughed.

"I told you I'd be watching you," Violet said to me. "What have you been up to?" she asked Albertina.

"Wait until you see!" Albertina said. I glared at her. I didn't want her telling Violet what we were doing, but she kept right on talking. "We're building a tree house at Molly's."

Violet looked interested. "Can I see?"

"No," I said at the same time Albertina said, "Sure." This time we did *not* have the same thought.

"Suit yourself," Violet said to me with a shrug. She moved closer to me, and I had to keep my feet from running away with me.

"Don't think I won't see it when I want to," she said as she ran off.

"Molly, that wasn't very nice," said Albertina.

"No," I said happily. "It wasn't."

"But she's my friend," said Albertina.

"Well, she's not mine," I said as we reached Albertina's gate. "See you tomorrow, Albertina."

I thought about Violet as I walked back home. Once I thought I heard someone in the bushes. It might have been a cat, but I decided to walk a little faster just in case.

Saturday we worked all day and finished the floor of the tree house. It was so strong even Mom and Dad could stand on it. Walter wanted to come up, too, so Dad handed him up to Mom, and Walter wiggled and made spit bubbles and smiled.

"He likes it," said Albertina. Walter looked at her and made a face. Albertina laughed and Walter laughed back.

"He likes you," said Mom.

"We all like you," I said, and Albertina smiled.

It's true, I thought to myself. Albertina was a perfect friend.

"Well, the rest is going to be up to you," said Grandpa.

Mom and Dad looked worried.

"We need to talk about this," said Dad.

"I'm not sure the girls should work up there by themselves," said Mom. "What if they fall?"

"You worry too much," Grandpa said. "It's not that high, and I've worked with them all day. They're good, safe workers."

"I'd feel better if they wore helmets," Mom said.

"Mom!" I said.

"Well, I would."

"Grandpa," I pleaded. "Make them listen."

Grandpa shrugged. "I've said all I can say."

I could tell he thought helmets were a silly idea.

"I have an idea," Dad said. "What if we make an agreement that there's no working on the tree house unless one of us is at home and knows you're up there? That way we'll know to keep more of an eye on you."

I didn't like it, but it was better than bike helmets in a tree, for heaven's sake.

"Maybe we should make sure this is okay with Albertina's father, too," said Mom.

"Can I invite my dad to see how the tree house is coming?" asked Albertina.

"Of course," said Mom. "How about having a picnic?"

"Great," I said. "Can Albertina and I eat in the tree house?"

"I don't know," said Daddy. "There aren't any walls yet."

"We'll be careful!" Albertina said.

"Please?" I begged.

Dad looked at Mom. "What do you say?"

"Oh, all right," said Mom, "as long as they don't drop their food on the rest of us."

"Mom!"

Mom laughed. "Now go ask Albertina's dad if he's up for a picnic tonight."

He was. Albertina and I helped make dinner, and Albertina's father brought ice cream.

"Hope everyone likes chocolate," he said when he showed up.

Walter dropped his stuffed bear and stared. He'd never heard someone with such a low, rumbling voice. Every time Albertina's father spoke, Walter stopped whatever he was doing and looked at him.

"I'm not sure I can eat with this much attention," said Albertina's father.

Of course that made Walter stop blowing spit bubbles again just to look at the big, tall stranger with the deep voice.

It made everybody laugh, and Albertina's father laughed most of all.

"Our first dinner in the tree house," Albertina said with a smile.

We spied on everybody talking and laughing below. A song sparrow sang in a branch of our tree. Albertina's dad heard it and said that meant good luck for our new tree house. I hugged myself, I was so happy.

Albertina and I wanted to sleep in the tree house, but all the grown-ups agreed we couldn't do that until the walls were built.

"Then can Molly spend the night at my house?" Albertina asked.

"Sure," said Mom, before I could say, "Let's do it here."

Mom knew I hated spending the night at anyone else's house. She probably figured it would be good for me. How good could it be when I wouldn't be sleeping at all, I'd like to know. She knows I can't sleep in the dark.

Of course I didn't say any of this.

"Cool," I said instead.

I almost reminded Albertina about my being scared of the dark, but I just couldn't do it. I'd been embarrassed enough telling her the first time. Besides, even though I wished she'd remember, I also kind of hoped she'd forgotten. I decided I'd just have to make the best of it.

"Your first overnight at my house!" Albertina said when we got my sleeping bag and pajamas. "I'm so excited! This will be a night to remember."

I had a sinking feeling she was right.

.5.
The Long Night

Albertina acted so happy about our overnight that for a while I thought it might be okay. Maybe I wouldn't get scared. Maybe she slept with the door open and the hall light on. Maybe she'd gotten a night-light just for fun.

No such luck.

Albertina's room was perfectly tidy, of course, but there was no night-light in sight. I didn't say anything about night-lights, but the room was another story.

"Do me a favor, Albertina," I said. "Never let my mom see your room!"

"How come?" she asked.

"Because I've almost convinced her that all kids are messy. Your room would sink me for sure."

"It would?" She looked surprised.

"Well, sure, Albertina," I said, rolling out my sleeping bag. "Just look at this place. We don't even have to move stuff around to make room for our sleeping bags."

"What should I do?" Albertina frowned.

"Don't worry, Albertina," I said. "I won't tell anyone. You have many other fine qualities."

We both laughed at that. As Albertina turned out the light and I crawled into my sleeping bag, I couldn't help wishing that one of Albertina's fine qualities was remembering my fear of the dark. Maybe she'd remember once we were both curled up in our sleeping bags. I crossed my fingers, but I knew there wasn't much hope.

She didn't leave the door open, and I couldn't see any light under the door. How could she stand it? It gave me the creeps.

Maybe it seemed spooky to Albertina, too, because suddenly she said, "Molly, I have an idea."

I hoped her idea had something to do with turning on lights, but it didn't.

"Let's tell ghost stories," she said.

No way! I thought. I pretended to consider the idea, though.

"How about telling stories from when we were little instead?"

"Okay," said Albertina. At least she didn't insist on following her own ideas.

I was fine as long as we were talking. I think Albertina fell asleep during the story of my third birthday party. When I realized she wasn't

listening and wasn't going to wake up until morning, I knew I was in trouble.

I tried to sleep, but my heart kept thumping. It didn't help that the pipes in her house made strange clanging noises. At least I hoped they were just pipes.

I practiced slow breathing, the way my dad taught me. I couldn't sleep. I tried counting, too, until I got so high up the numbers confused me. Still I couldn't sleep. I said all the prayers I'd learned at Sunday school, and finally I started falling asleep.

Then something rustled in the closet.

I sat straight up, wide awake. "Albertina," I whispered, in case she was pretending to sleep. She wasn't.

Should I wake her up? I couldn't just let her sleep when the something in her closet might jump out and get her at any moment.

"Albertina," I whispered again. Nothing.

Well, maybe I should wait until I had figured

out just what the something in her closet was. That would be easier to explain. So I tried hard to listen, but by now I couldn't hear a thing. My heart pounded so hard it drummed out every other sound. I could even hear it  pounding in my ears. I tried holding my breath, but I still couldn't hear anything.

By the time my heart quieted down, whatever was in the closet must have fallen asleep, because it wasn't making any more noise. I hoped it would sleep all night. Maybe now I could sleep.

But no. Now I needed to go to the bathroom. I couldn't do it. I couldn't walk through that dark room out into the dark hall in Albertina's dark, strange house.

I waited. Why didn't morning come?

Finally I couldn't wait another minute. I got

out of my sleeping bag ever so quietly. I tried to sneak to the door so whatever was probably waiting on the other side wouldn't hear me coming and be ready to snatch me the minute I opened the door. I opened the door very slowly so I could catch whatever was on the other side by surprise.

Eeeee! The door squeaked, and I screamed, and that woke up Albertina, who yelled. The next thing I knew, her dad ran into the room.

"What's going on in here?" he asked. "It's two o'clock in the morning!"

"Ask her," said Albertina.

"I'm sorry," I said. "I was just getting up to go to the bathroom, and something surprised me."

"Something surprised you?" asked Albertina's father.

"I mean I thought something surprised me," I said, feeling foolish.

"Well, you surprised me," said Albertina. "I'm going back to sleep."

But when I came back from the bathroom, Albertina was still awake.

"Molly, were you scared of the dark just now?"

I didn't answer.

"I'm sorry, Molly. I forgot you didn't like the dark. Why didn't you remind me?"

"It's all right," I said.

"We can open the door," said Albertina. "I'll turn on the hall light."

On the way back, she opened a desk drawer and pulled out a big yellow flashlight. "Here, take this," she said. "It can be your blanket," she said with a laugh. "That's what I sleep with."

"A blanket?"

"Yeah," said Albertina. "See?" She pulled out a ragged pink quilt. "I can sleep without it, but I sleep better with it."

"Thanks, Albertina," I said as we settled back into our

sleeping bags. I stuck the flashlight under my pillow, closed my eyes, and fell asleep.

The next morning Albertina's father didn't mention getting woken up. I decided he was a pretty nice man. He made us pancakes with real apple butter. I ate six pancakes, and Albertina ate seven!

"You girls will be so heavy you'll knock that poor tree house down," Albertina's father teased.

"We're going to need a lot of energy for work today," I told him.

Albertina borrowed some tools from her dad, and we went back to my house to start putting up walls.

"I hope we can sleep in it before school starts," Albertina said.

"Me, too," I agreed. "Maybe we'll finish the walls today."

Building walls turned out to be a lot harder than we expected, especially in the hot sun. We followed Grandpa's plans, but boards kept falling over.

"I think I've pounded a thousand nails," said Albertina.

"Same here," I said.

By the end of the day, all we had up was part of one wall.

"Don't give up," said Dad. "It always takes longer than you think to build something, especially when you're doing such a good job."

"Do you really think we're doing a good job?" Albertina asked.

"Of course I do," said Dad. "I mean what I say and I say what I mean."

"Hey, just like me," said Albertina. "That's what I always say."

She and Dad looked at each other. I could tell that they were both pleased.

.6.
Baby-sitter!

Some days you wake up and know it will be a good day. This wasn't one of those days. Even before breakfast, I could tell something was up.

"Good morning, honey," said Mom.

Mom never calls me honey unless she is trying to get on my good side. I sat down and poured myself some cereal.

"Guess what?" said Dad.

Here it comes, I thought.

"I get to go to Japan for a couple weeks," he said.

"Japan! What about me and Walter?"

Dad usually works at home and takes care of us kids. When he traveled before, Grandma and Grandpa took care of us while Mom worked. Now that we didn't live together, I didn't know what we'd do.

"Will Grandma and Grandpa come over?" I asked.

"No," said Dad. "Since it's summer, we thought we'd just get a teenager to come over while Mom's at work."

"A baby-sitter!"

"Now, Molly," said Mom. "Albertina has a baby-sitter, and it doesn't seem to bother her."

"Mary is a housekeeper," I said. "She just happens to keep an eye on Albertina."

"Housekeeper or baby-sitter, we have already found somebody, and she seems very nice. Her name is Kathy, and she lives in the white house with green trim right up the street."

"But that's Violet's house," I said. "She must be Violet's sister!"

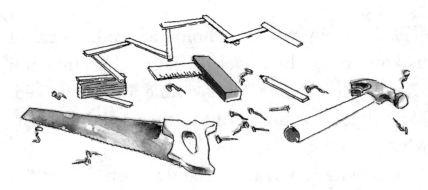

"Yes," said Dad. "I think she said that. She might even bring Violet over some morning. It would be nice if you had someone besides Albertina to play with."

"I don't want someone besides Albertina to play with! I don't even have time to play with my *old* friends." Dad started to interrupt, but I kept talking. "Dad, listen! Violet is the girl who tried to scare me when we first moved here. How could you?"

"Calm down, Molly," said Mom, but I didn't.

"Even if I did want a monster in the house, Albertina and I are too busy. We want to finish the tree house before school starts."

"That reminds me, Molly," Mom said. "No

working on the tree house when Kathy's here."

"You can't mean that!" I said. "We have to work on the tree house!"

"You remember our agreement," Mom said. "No tree house when your father and I are both gone. It's not fair to the baby-sitter. Too many things could go wrong."

"Besides," said Dad, "Kathy will need your help with Walter. You know he's starting to get shy around strangers."

Great. Now instead of building a tree house, I got to hang out and baby-sit with the sister of the neighborhood monster. "Wait until Albertina hears about this," I said.

My parents didn't look worried.

"The worst thing is happening," I told Albertina when she came over after breakfast.

"You're not moving, are you?"

"Not that," I said. "But it's almost as bad." I told her all about it while we got tools out of the shed.

"It'll be okay, Molly," she said.

"Do you have to be so cheerful about everything, Albertina?" I wanted her to be mad, too.

"Sorry," she said. "I was just trying to help."

"Nothing will help," I said.

"But, Molly, can't we still work on it when your mom comes home?"

"Yes," I said, "but we won't be through by the time school starts."

"As long as we're done before it snows, I'll be happy," said Albertina.

"What do you know about this Kathy?"
I asked.

"Oh, you'll like Kathy," Albertina said.

"Is she insecure like her sister?" I asked. I hadn't forgotten Albertina's excuse for Violet.

"You're so funny, Molly," Albertina said. "Kathy took care of me last summer, before Mary started coming. Kathy is kind of boy crazy, but she's nice and she lets you do almost anything."

"Maybe she'll let us work on the tree house anyway."

Albertina shook her head. "No," she said. "She won't let you do something your parents have forbidden. Besides, you and I made an agreement with your parents."

"I suppose," I said.

"She'll let you do anything else, though," Albertina said. "You'll still have fun."

"Will you still come over and play?"

"Sure I will," said Albertina. "Maybe Kathy will bring Violet, too."

"I don't want to play with Violet," I said. "I mean it."

"You should give her another chance, Molly."

"Not this year," I said.

Albertina laughed and, after a minute, I laughed, too.

"When does your dad leave?" asked Albertina.

"Next week," I said.

"Then we'd better stop talking and get to work."

.7.
Enemy in the Camp

I always missed Dad when he left, but I was *really* sorry to see him go this time. The next morning Kathy came over before Mom went to work. At least she didn't bring Violet.

"Walter is shy of strangers," Mom told Kathy as she walked out the door. "Molly will play with him until he gets used to you. I think it would be a good idea if she didn't have any friends over this first day."

No friends! I called Albertina to give her the bad news.

When Walter went down for his morning

nap, Kathy said, "Why don't you show me your room?"

Great. Violet's sister looking at my things, reporting on my stuff. I couldn't believe it. Suddenly I thought about my night-light. I ran into my room ahead of her, grabbed my night-light and stuck it in a drawer. At least that would remain a secret. There was no hiding the mess, though.

"I've been too busy to clean lately," I said.

Kathy didn't seem shocked. "Looks just like my sister's room," she said.

That was interesting. Maybe it was even one point in Violet's favor.

We didn't hang around in my room, though. The phone rang, and Kathy raced to answer it. She was hoping it was her boyfriend, but it was only Mom checking on how things were going.

Once Walter got up from his nap, I spent the rest of the morning stacking blocks on top of one another while Walter knocked them down.

He gurgled and grinned.

"Just wait until you get older," I told him. "You're going to owe me for this."

Meanwhile Kathy talked to her boyfriend on the phone. Then she read a magazine. Then she talked to her boyfriend again.

"Maybe you should pay *me*," I told Mom when she came home that night. "The only time I got a break was when Walter took his nap."

"Chin up," said Mom.

Albertina came over after dinner, and we worked on the tree house.

"What did you do today?" I asked.

"Daddy told Mary I had to clean my room."

"You're kidding. What did it take? Five minutes?"

"Don't be silly, Molly," said Albertina. "It took all morning."

I guess I'll never completely understand Albertina.

"What did you do the rest of the day?" I asked.

"I played with Violet," Albertina said.

"Violet!"

"What's wrong with that?" Albertina asked. "Just because you don't like her doesn't mean I can't like her."

I knew she was right, but it still made me mad. It wasn't even dark yet when I said, "Let's call it quits. I'm tired."

I was more mad than tired. Albertina didn't argue, though.

"See you tomorrow," she said.

"Maybe," I said.

Albertina didn't come over at all the next day.

I called her before I went to bed.

"Please come over tomorrow, Albertina," I said. "I miss you when you're not here."

So she came and played with me and Walter while Kathy read magazines. We took Walter for a walk in the stroller. We made milk shakes for lunch. Kathy didn't care what we did as long as she didn't have to do anything.

The next few days were all about the same. Albertina and I played with Walter and waited for Mom to come home so we could work on the tree house.

Then one morning when Kathy came, I heard my mom say, "Oh, what a nice surprise. I think you're just my daughter Molly's age." This could only mean one thing. "Come with me," I heard her say. My own mother!

I grabbed my night-light off the wall just in the nick of time. Mom had her hand on Violet's shoulder and was walking into my room without even knocking!

"Look who's here, Molly," said Mom.

I made a noise that I thought was pretty close to hello, but I guess Mom didn't agree.

She glared at me. I glared back. "Molly," she said in kind of a warning tone, "Violet is spending the morning here today."

Violet stared at everything in my room, her eyes focused like X rays, trying to discover my secrets. I could tell.

"We can't stay in here," I said, walking out the door and motioning them to follow. I closed the door behind me, hard.

I could tell Mom was mad. She was probably biting her tongue to keep from telling me to behave myself. She just looked at her watch, though, and said, "I've got to go. Good-bye, girls."

"*Nobody* goes in my room without my permission," I told Violet after Mom left. "We can go in the living room and help Kathy with Walter."

Walter seemed to like Violet. Just goes to show how easy babies are to fool, that's what I figured.

I have to admit that it was nice having someone else to entertain Walter. Violet paid him more attention than her sister ever did, and I even got to read a book for a change. Kathy just talked on the phone, as usual. Every now and then Violet looked like she wanted to say something to me, but I always looked away. I wasn't going to fall for her tricks again.

"Why don't you show Violet your tree house?" Kathy asked when she finally got off the phone.

"Would you?" Violet asked, a little nervously, I thought.

I shrugged. "Suits me," I said, "but we're just looking. No climbing up in it." I didn't tell her that was because I wasn't allowed to when my parents were gone.

"Wow!" said Violet when she saw the tree house. "Two walls up! Albertina said it was going

to be a real house, but I thought she was exaggerating. You and Albertina did all this by yourselves?"

"Sure," I said, pretending it was no big deal. It was fun having Violet, the bully, look so longingly at my tree house. I didn't invite her to come back again, though. Eat your heart out, I thought, and I was glad when lunchtime came and Violet went back home. Still, she hadn't been as bad as I'd expected.

The rest of the time Dad was gone went pretty quickly. Albertina came over most days, and we worked on the tree house when Mom came home at night. Some days Albertina played with other kids, even Violet. I didn't complain about her friends anymore. She wanted to bring Violet over one day, but I said no.

"You can have your own friends," I said, "but that doesn't mean I have to like them."

"Fair enough," said Albertina.

I invited Kelley over one day and Bruce over twice. They liked the tree house from the outside, but they *really* liked it when Mom came home and they could climb up.

Still, when Dad got back, it was a big relief to everybody. Kathy had started getting on my nerves. Mom looked tired, too. Even Albertina gave Dad a hug.

"I'm sure glad you're back," she said. "School starts in a week, and Molly and I have a lot of work to do."

"Oh?" said Dad.

"We need to finish the walls before school starts," Albertina and I said at the same time.

I smiled. Things were back to normal.

.8.
School!

At last the tree house walls were up!

"It's looking good, girls," said Grandpa. He came over a lot to check on us.

"You should be very proud," Dad said.

"We are!" Albertina and I said together.

"The roof isn't up," said Dad, "but that shouldn't stop you from sleeping in it."

Albertina and I hugged each other, we were so excited.

We could hardly wait for bedtime. We had waited all summer for this.

"Summer is almost over," Albertina said as we crawled into our sleeping bags.

"I know," I said. "I didn't even know you when summer started. Isn't that amazing?"

Albertina nodded. We had spent so much time together the last few weeks, it seemed as if we had always been friends.

"Look, the first star," said Albertina. "Did you make a wish?"

I nodded. "I'm wishing we'll be in the same class," I said.

"Well, that's just what I wished, too," said Albertina.

"That must mean something," we said at the same time, and then rolled over laughing. The moon and stars lit the sky, so I didn't even miss my night-light. I had a flashlight with me just in case, and Albertina had her pink blanket.

We talked a long time about school and what it would be like.

"I just wish I knew a few more kids," I said.

"Don't worry," she said. "Everyone will like you, just like I do."

"Just like Violet?" I said.

"Oh, Violet," said Albertina with a snort. "I told you she was just insecure."

"I just hope the other kids aren't insecure, too!" I said.

Albertina laughed. "Don't worry Molly. I'll protect you. Now, good night."

"Good night," I said.

I knew I didn't need to be protected. I was as brave as anybody. It was still a great relief, though, when I found out Albertina and I would both be in Miss Aamot's class.

"I want to show you something," said Albertina, getting out the telephone book. "Look. Aa. She has the very first name in the phone book!"

"Wow!" I said. I'd never known anyone who started the telephone book. "But is she *nice*, Albertina?"

"The best," said Albertina. "Quit worrying."

On the first day of school Albertina came by to pick me up, and my dad walked us both down to the school.

"Have a great day," he said when he told us good-bye.

I saw Violet and a pack of girls just around the corner. Someone pointed at me, and I saw Violet say something to her. Well, I didn't care. She could say whatever she wanted. At least they left me alone.

Albertina was right about Miss Aamot. I liked her right away. I liked the other kids in the class, too.

Recess and lunch gave us time to play, and Violet even smiled at me once. Of course, she'd done that before. During the afternoon we played math bingo, and I won twice!

After school Albertina and I hurried home to work on the tree house some more.

"We've got to be done before it snows!" I said. "We only have a couple more months."

Every day after school we worked on the tree house, except on Tuesdays, when Albertina had Scouts, and Fridays, when I had piano lessons. Soon we had the roof on, although Mom had insisted on Dad hanging around while we worked on that.

On my birthday Grandpa gave me two presents. One was a roll of tar paper, and the other was a big box. Inside the box were real shingles—little pieces of wood to hammer onto our roof. "You'll have to let me help a little on this part," Grandpa said.

"It's a perfect present, Grandpa!" I gave him a big hug.

Albertina said, "I feel like I got a present, too."

Later that evening Albertina said, "Hey, I've got an idea. Let's try to finish the tree house by Halloween. Then we could have a haunted tree house."

"Albertina, you have more good ideas than anyone I know," I said, "except maybe for Grandpa."

"Thank you," said Albertina. "Are you still sorry you had to move here?"

"No, I am not," I said. "Moving here was the best thing that ever happened to me."

"Same here," said Albertina.

.9.

Betrayal

The tree house was almost finished. The shingles were up. The window holes were cut. Albertina and I had even started making window ledges. Every day brought us closer to our goal. During recess we planned what we'd do after school.

One day, while we were planning the afternoon's work, Flora called me.

"Molly, come over here!"

I left Albertina and ran to the swings where Flora and her twin, Frederick, were playing. Frederick handed me an invitation to their birthday party.

"Thanks," I said. I knew Albertina had been invited, and now we could go together.

As I walked back over to the climber I saw Albertina talking to Violet. They looked very serious, and when I got close, I heard Albertina say, "Her mother bought it for her. It's just like a rocket ship."

Albertina! I couldn't believe my ears. Albertina, my very best friend, the most perfect person I knew, was telling Violet about my night-light! Boy, had she fooled me.

I turned around and ran straight into the school.

For the rest of the day I stayed away from Albertina. I didn't look at her. I didn't talk to her. When Albertina asked me what was wrong, I ignored her.

When school ended, I grabbed my jacket and ran home without even putting it on. I was crying so hard I could hardly see.

"Where's Albertina?" Dad asked when I got home.

"Don't ask me!" I said.

I guess Dad could tell I'd been crying, because he picked up Walter and followed me into my room.

"What's wrong?"

"Nothing!" I shouted. "Nothing is wrong. I just came home alone. Aren't I allowed to do that anymore?"

My shouting made Walter cry, and then I felt worse.

"We should talk about this, Molly," Dad said over the noise of Walter's howls. "Later, okay?"

"Just leave me alone!" I hollered. I lay down on my bed and cried some more.

After a while I decided maybe working on the
tree house would make me feel better. It did, at
least until Mom came home.

"Hello up there," she called.

I stopped hammering and looked over the side.

"Hi, Mom."

"Where's Albertina?" she asked, just like Dad.

"How should I know?"

Mom looked surprised. "She's usually up there,
and she is your best friend," she said.

"She *was* my best friend," I said. "Now Sylvia is."

I jumped out of the tree and followed Mom into the house.

Mom laughed. "Don't be silly, Molly. Sylvia is a goldfish," she said, as if I didn't know.

I glared at her. She went into the kitchen.

A few minutes later I heard the phone ring. "Molly, Violet is on the phone," Mom called, as if it were the most natural thing in the world for Violet to call. Violet! Calling to gloat, no doubt.

I picked up the phone. "Wrong number," I said, and hung up. I went into my room to check my building plans and to talk to Sylvia.

"You have a big mouth," I told her, "but you don't use it to tell secrets like some people I could name."

Sylvia opened and closed her mouth. She understood me perfectly. I was glad someone did.

.10.

Miserable

In the morning Albertina came by to pick me up as usual.

"Is Molly here?" she asked my dad.

"Shh," I whispered to Sylvia. Sylvia never breathed a word while I grabbed my lunch box and ran out the back door. I ran all the way to school and never looked back.

Albertina got to school a few minutes after I did. She waved when she saw me. I looked away.

During art time Miss Aamot said, "Draw a picture of you and your best friend together."

Albertina drew a picture of her and me working on the tree house.

I drew a picture of Sylvia and me watching television.

Albertina looked surprised when she saw my picture. She quit smiling, too.

On the playground at lunchtime I could hear Albertina laughing over by the monkey bars. Everyone around her laughed, too. You can't help it with Albertina. It's one of the things I had always liked so much about her. But now I stayed away from the monkey bars.

"Molly. Can I talk to you?"

It was Violet. Another trick. I hurried away and joined Frederick and Flora on the sandpile.

We played King of the Mountain during the rest of lunch. I didn't actually have much fun. Flora cried when I got to the top of the sandpile first. What a bad sport! I could still hear Albertina's laugh—Albertina, who never cared who won.

After school I walked home with William, a boy in my class.

"Can I see your tree house?" he asked.

"Sure," I said. There was no reason to keep it all to myself.

"Grandpa helped me and Albertina with the floor and the roof," I told William, "but we did everything else ourselves." I could tell he was impressed.

"Can I help?" he asked.

"Why not?" I said. After all, I was going to need some help now that I was through with Albertina.

But William was no help at all. He fussed over which hammer he used. Then when I let him use the big one, he hit his finger with it and started to cry. Finally he just went home.

Good riddance, I thought. Albertina never fought over the tools, and she was a whole lot better than William at using a hammer. But Albertina wasn't around. She'd gone home with Violet—not that it mattered to me.

I tried sawing a board in half. It was pretty hard keeping it steady and sawing it all by myself. I got disgusted and gave up.

"Are you all right?" Dad asked when he saw me putting away tools. "Do you want to talk?"

I could tell he was worried. "I'm okay," I said. "I'm just going in the house for a while."

"Hi, Sylvia," I said to my best friend when I went in my room. She opened her mouth and closed it again.

"It wasn't a very good day," I continued. Sylvia didn't look too concerned. I couldn't help

remembering that Albertina always felt bad when I did. Sylvia just opened and closed her mouth some more.

"I miss Albertina," I told Sylvia as I fed her a snack. "But don't tell anyone." At least I knew Sylvia would keep my secret, unlike some people.

It was a mistake, letting myself think about Albertina. I wanted to call and ask her to come over and help me finish the tree house, but how could I after what she'd done? This was even worse than Violet trying to scare me when I moved in. After all, Albertina was my best friend! I started crying.

"How could she tell Violet?" I asked Sylvia. "It was a secret!" Sylvia swam behind her castle. I wasn't sure she even cared that I was crying. Some best friend. I cried harder.

I didn't have the heart to work on the tree house the rest of the day. I cleaned the fishbowl instead and just sat around the house. Moping, Mom called it. I knew it was a broken heart.

.11.

Albertina the Practically Perfect

That night after dinner the doorbell rang.

"Molly," yelled Mom. "You have company."

Albertina walked into the room before I had a chance to escape. She looked awful.

"Why is your face so puffy and red?" I asked her.

"Why is yours?" she asked me back.

We both stood there and sniffled.

"Why don't you like me anymore?" Albertina asked, finally.

"I can't trust you," I said. "You told Violet that I sleep with a night-light."

"You do sleep with a night-light," said Albertina.

"Yes, but now she's going to think I'm scared of the dark," I said.

"But you are scared of the dark," Albertina said.

"That's supposed to be a secret!" I shouted. "You had no business telling everyone."

"Nobody cares if you're scared of the dark," Albertina said. "Besides, I didn't tell everyone. I only told Violet."

"She'll probably tell the whole neighborhood. I'm ruined."

"Molly, Violet is afraid of the dark, too. I told her about your rocket ship night-light. She's going to ask her mom to get her one, too."

"Violet, the toughest, meanest kid on the block, is scared of the dark? I don't believe you."

"That's just what Violet said. 'I don't believe you. I've seen her working up on that tree house. I bet she's not scared of anything.'"

"Really? Violet said that?"

"Yes," Albertina sniffed. "She *likes* you, Molly. She wants to be friends."

That was hard to believe, too. "Are you sure?"

"Yes. She's really sorry she acted so mean when you first came. She never knew you would hold it against her forever. She thought maybe when she came over to your house with Kathy, you'd see that she was ready to be friends. Look how much you two are alike."

"Me and Violet?" That was a strange thought.

"Sure. You're both strong and smart. You're both tough. You both have messy rooms." That almost made me laugh. "And," Albertina added, "you're both scared of the dark!"

Okay. She had a point. And Violet really hadn't been all that bad the day she'd come over, and she did act friendly at school.

"It was still my secret, Albertina. You said you wouldn't tell. You didn't tell the truth. Even if you had a good reason, you should have asked me first."

Albertina looked like she was going to cry again. "I'm sorry," she said. "I won't do it again. I made a mistake. Please, can we still be friends?"

I looked at Sylvia just swimming in the bowl. I thought about working all alone on the tree house, or, worse, working with William. I thought about Flora crying just because I was King of the Mountain. And I thought about everybody happy and laughing on the playground just because Albertina was around.

"Sure, Albertina," I said. I couldn't help smiling. "You're more fun than anybody."

"Even though I'm not perfect?" she asked.

I laughed. "I'll get used to it."

Dad opened the door and peeked in. "Everything okay in here?"

"Everything's great," Albertina and I said, at the very same time.

"You're doing it again!" Dad said, and we all laughed.

"Hey, why are we standing around in here?" Albertina asked. "We've got a tree house to finish!"